To Lisa, the ultimate Mommy Doo!
I love you, yes I do.

Special thanks to Katonah Elementary School
and to Lewisboro Elementary School

Photography by Sandra Kress

Digital coloring and compositing by Paul Zdanowicz

"New Kid in Class" song by Dan Sawyer, ASCAP. Used by permission.

www.stepintoreading.com

Educators and librarians, for a variety of teaching tools, visit us at
www.randomhouse.com/teachers

Library of Congress Cataloging-in-Publication Data
Jinkins, Jim.
Shrinky Pinky! / written and illustrated by Jim Jinkins. — 1st ed.
    p. cm. — (Step into reading) "Step into reading: Pinky Dinky Doo."
SUMMARY: Pinky Dinky Doo, an imaginative young girl, tells her brother a story about how she had to deal with a bully.
ISBN 0-375-83234-3 (hardcover) — ISBN 0-375-83235-1 (trade) — ISBN 0-375-93235-6 (lib. bdg.)
[1. Bullies—Fiction. 2. Brothers and sisters—Fiction. 3. Storytelling—Fiction. 4. Imagination—Fiction.] I. Title. II. Series.
PZ7.J57526Sh 2005   [E]—dc22   2004006101

Printed in the United States of America   10 9 8 7 6 5 4 3 2 1

Pinky Dinky Doo™

SHRRINKY PINKY!

by Jim Jinkins

Random House 🏠 New York

Mommy Doo

Daddy Doo

Mr. Guinea Pig

Tyler Doo

Pinky Dinky Doo

Nicholas Biscuit

Daffinee Toilette

Introducing
Lane Puppytray

Bobby Boom

"Sure, little brother,"

Pinky said.

"What happened to your nose?"

"It ran into Johnny Gelona's

fist today,"

Tyler said.

"Sounds like you have

a problem on your hands,"

said Pinky.

"More like on my nose,"

Tyler said.

"Okay, Tyler!

I'm going to tell you a story

about someone so mean

he almost ate Great Big City!"

"I'll just shut my eyes,

wiggle my ears,

and crank up my imagination,"
Pinky said.

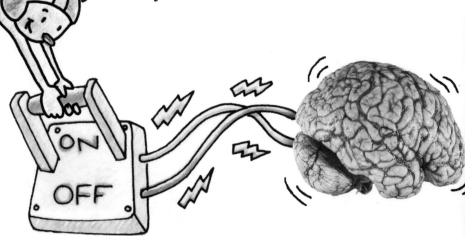

"The name of this story is . . ."

A made-up story
by Pinky Dinky Doo

That's DINKY!

9

It was a normal day
in music class . . .

until Ms. La Deedah,

the music teacher,

told the class a NEW KID

(a girl) was joining them.

"I wonder what

she'll be like,"

Pinky said.

"I heard she's from out of state,"
said Daffinee Toilette.

"I heard she's from outer space!"
said Ross Applesauce.

The whole class started buzzing
at the idea of a slimy,
gross alien in music class.

Then the new kid came into the room.

She wasn't slimy or gross.

She was a cute girl in capri pants,

who smelled like flowers.

"Class,"

said Ms. La Deedah,

"this is Lane Puppytray."

Lane seemed nice.

She played the recorder!

She knew "The Caterpillar Song."

She could even play

"The Pickle Barrel Polka"!

Pinky thought Lane
was fun and different
and exciting.
She had climbed
Mount Hunky-Dory.

She had explored the
Woolly Mammoth Caves.

She had even
visited the sun!

Hey, how did she go to the sun without burning up?

She traveled at night!

Then one day Pinky Dinky Doo
heard Abby McTabby
talking about Lane Puppytray.
Abby said Lane was bossy.

Sometimes she's even mean!

In the cafeteria,
Pinky saw it for herself.
Lane jumped in line
right in front of her!

Mrs. Tartarsauce,

the cafeteria lady,

thought she saw what had happened.

She frowned at

Pinky and said,

"Go to the back

of the line."

"But—"

Pinky began.

"No buts,

Miss Doo!

You've done enough butting."

Pinky was so mad.

Things got worse and worse.

During the next week, Lane . . .

A Broke Pinky's favorite pen.

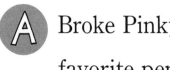

Lane

B Took Pinky's homework.

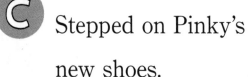

C Stepped on Pinky's new shoes.

D All of the above.

Unfortunately for Pinky, the answer is **D**, all of the above.

Ooh . . . harsh.

"Lane is a . . .

what's a word for someone

as mean as a WARTHOG

with poison ivy?

Johnny
Gelona?

A bully—

that's the word,"

said Pinky.

Pinky *had*

to make Lane stop

picking on her.

She trudged home after school.
She looked at
Mr. Guinea Pig.
He was lucky.

"He's so small,"
  Pinky said.
"A bully wouldn't even notice him."
  Then Pinky had an idea.

"Maybe I can shrink myself down to the size of Mr. Guinea Pig. If Lane can't see me, she can't pick on me." But how could Pinky make herself shrink?

She put a heavy book on her head.

But that just mashed down her hair.

She tried the old "put your shoes

on your knees" trick.

Your knees go in a big
pair of your dad's shoes.

Hide legs
under chair.

Kids, try this at home!

But it was hard
to get around that way.

Slide at school
playground.

Then Pinky remembered one time
when Daddy Doo did the laundry.
He washed her dress in hot water
and dried it too long.
It shrank to a tiny size.

So Pinky hopped in the shower
(clothes and all).

Then she stood under the heater.

Pinky felt herself getting smaller.

She shrank

and
shrank

and
shrank.

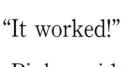

"It worked!"

Pinky said in a tiny voice.

Now she had to find out

if being so tiny

would keep Lane

from bugging her.

But how could she get

to Lane's house?

Then Pinky had the best idea.

She climbed inside Mr. Guinea Pig's exercise ball and rolled over there.

Lane was hanging around, reading a magazine.

Use your finger to find the way.

Pinky got out of the ball.

"Yoo-hoo . . . Lane!

I'm down here,"

she shouted.

But Lane never saw her.

"Being little is great!"

Pinky said.

She wanted to tell someone about it.

Pinky rolled home and went
to find Mr. Guinea Pig.

Pinky got into Mr. Guinea Pig's cage.

She peeked inside his box.

Wowee!

Mr. Guinea Pig
had a nice pad!

A fire was burning in the fireplace.
There was music playing that
made Pinky feel like dancing.

Mr. Guinea Pig came
out of the kitchen.
He was wearing a fancy robe
and slippers and was sipping
some lemonade.

Mr. G. poured Pinky some lemonade.

Then Pinky told him

about her problem with Lane.

"I need to THINK BIG,"

said Mr. G.

"I didn't know you could talk,"

Pinky said.

"I talk all the time," he said.

"You just can't hear me."

Mr. Guinea Pig began to think.

Normally, Mr. G. had an everyday,

guinea pig–sized brain.

But not when he decided

to THINK BIG.

He thought and thought and thought!

And his little guinea-pig brain

got bigger and bigger,

until his head filled up

the whole room.

And then it happened . . .

Mr. Guinea Pig had a big idea.

"I know what you can do!"

Mr. Guinea Pig said.

"You can . . .

A Peel grapes for me and rub my toes.

B Shrink even more and join the flea circus.

C Become big Pinky again and really figure this thing out."

I can do this!

Pinky knew that the answer was **C**, of course.

Now Mr. G. had another big idea.

He scanned Pinky into his computer and enlarged her to normal size.

SIZE / 100%

Pinky was back to her old self.
And she realized
something important.

"I have great friends like
Mr. Guinea Pig and Daffinee
and Nicholas," said Pinky.
"So, if *Lane* wants to be my friend,
she'll have to act like one."

"And if she doesn't,
I'll just have to put her
on a rocket ship
to planet Bully B. Gone,"
Pinky said.

"Once Lane figured out

she couldn't boss me around,

I was much happier.

And she got nicer . . . eventually."

"And that's exactly what happened . . .

pretty much,"

Pinky said to Tyler.

POOF!

"The end."

"Hey!" said Tyler.

"What happened to the mean person who almost ate Great Big City?"

"Oh yeah," Pinky said.

"Then there was some other guy who almost ate Great Big City. The end."

"You cheated!"
Tyler said.
He hit Pinky
with a pillow.
Pinky was shocked.

"Tyler,
are you being a bully?"
Pinky asked.
Tyler stopped.
"I'm just being
a little brother,"
he said.

"In that case,"

said Pinky . . .

"pillow fight!"